I0732576

TONY PANG

Taqwah Travels:
Jassasah's Cave

First published by MESAI Global LLC 2022

Copyright © 2022 by Tony Pang

All rights reserved. No part of this publication may be reproduced, stored or transmitted in any form or by any means, electronic, mechanical, photocopying, recording, scanning, or otherwise without written permission from the publisher. It is illegal to copy this book, post it to a website, or distribute it by any other means without permission.

This novel is entirely a work of fiction. The names, characters and incidents portrayed in it are the work of the author's imagination. Any resemblance to actual persons, living or dead, events or localities is entirely coincidental.

Tony Pang asserts the moral right to be identified as the author of this work.

Tony Pang has no responsibility for the persistence or accuracy of URLs for external or third-party Internet Websites referred to in this publication and does not guarantee that any content on such Websites is, or will remain, accurate or appropriate.

Designations used by companies to distinguish their products are often claimed as trademarks. All brand names and product names used in this book and on its cover are trade names, service marks, trademarks and registered trademarks of their respective owners. The publishers and the book are not associated with any product or vendor mentioned in this book. None of the companies referenced within the book have endorsed the book.

First edition

ISBN: 978-1-959133-04-9

This book was professionally typeset on Reedsy.
Find out more at reedsy.com

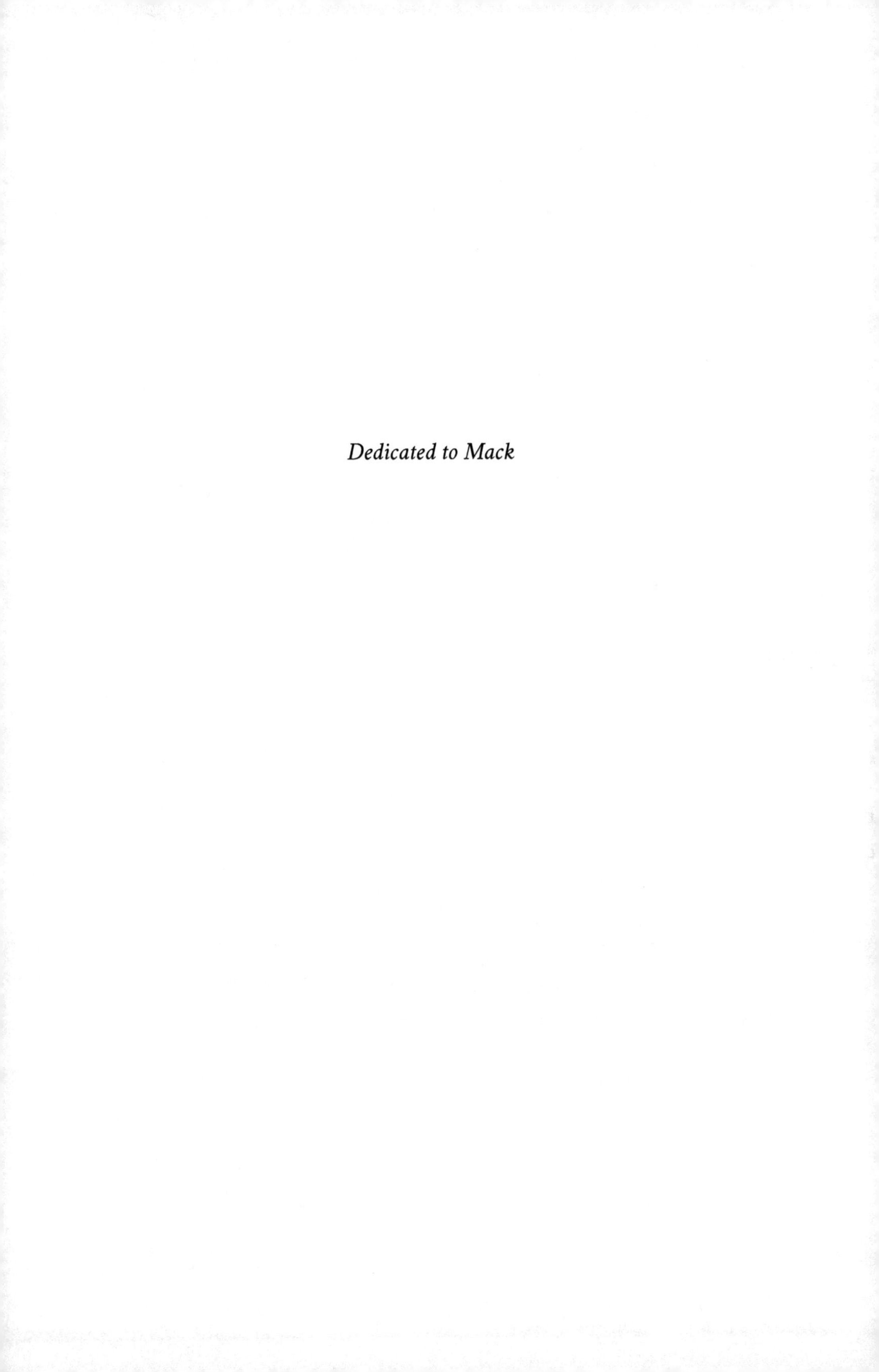

Dedicated to Mack

Above all else, guard your heart, for everything
you do flows from it.

Sulaimān ibn Dāwūd (A)

Contents

Acknowledgement

I'd like to start by thanking Allah (SWT), for giving me everything

I'd like to thank my mom, who was the main inspiration behind this story. *"You are the wind beneath my wings"*

Thank you Kareemah for checking my grammar and giving encouragement and support to keep me going.

thank you, my lovely readers, you followed me and stayed with me from Arabian Pirate to Turquoise Moon and I hope you enjoy The Hyena Hunt.

Finally, I can't leave without expressing my gratitude to everyone over at JustWrite who made this book what it is today. I do not know what I would do without you guys!

If you enjoyed this story, then please be sure to show your appreciation by leaving a review on either Amazon or Goodreads. It would mean more than I can express!

The Jassasah Cave

MESAI Adventures

By Tony Pang

Glossary

Malve – name of a river the dead must cross to reach the underworld

Quadriremes – a ship with two rows of oars

Marid – name of the ferryman who ships the dead across the River Malve

Benaiah – a soldier in the Al Sham army

Endongo – A stringed instrument like a small U or V shape harp with strings fixed to a crossbar used especially in ancient East Africa

Rofe – the Hebrew word for a doctor

Sho'er – the Hebrew word for a doorman

Kubwa – great, excellent, genuine

Senate – place where senators meet to make laws

Senator – a member of the senate

Welcome to a new adventure

Did you think you've seen all the dangers that there are? That's what Ibraheem and Menalik thought too! They have to face fresh challenges and dangers as they leave behind their home and those they love. Why? Because Princess Zaria has given Ibraheem and Menalik a CHALLENGE!

Will they rise up to the challenge of this adventure? Little do they know, but they will need all their courage to face the most terrifying danger in the whole world if they want to save a friend and themselves. Can you guess what this danger is…?

Read on to see how your hero's fare.

Chapter 1

Ibraheem, Menalik and their Zazzau friend Princess Zaria came through time and space in a whirl of stars.

"A cruise with Sulaimān Ibn Dāwūd (A) (King Solomon) and Queen Sheba!" Ibraheem said in outrage. "You couldn't have found anything harder to do."

Zaria smiled happily. "I've always wanted to see Sulaimān (A) and Sheba and now we can go on a cruise with them together. Maybe we'll go up the river Jordan. That would be so romantic."

Ibraheem banged his forehead with his hand in exasperation.

"I don't want to go on a cruise," he said. "I want to go home and…"

"Of course, you want to go on an adventure. You told me how much fun and how exciting your other adventures were. And just imagine meeting Sulaimān (A) and Sheba!"

"There's no ship here," Menalik said. "Just a long road."

He looked up and down the road. It was a straight cobbled Al Sham road and it was very long. In each direction the road stretched out all the way to the horizon. On both sides of the road was an area of grass, which Solomon's army kept short so there was no place for bandits to hide, followed by bushes and trees.

"Yes, it does look like a long way to walk," Zaria said as she realized that they weren't anywhere near a river, let alone a ship.

"Welcome to another Kubwa adventure," Ibraheem said sarcastically.

Zaria laughed happily. She was always a cheerful and optimistic person.

"Oh, come on," she said. "Things will be just fine and I'm sure we're going to have lots of fun together. But let's not stand around here or we'll never get anywhere. What direction shall we go?"

They looked in both directions, but everything looked the same.

"I wish I knew where we were," Menalik said.

The sun was high in the sky and it was hot, though not as hot as in Zazzau. The air was dry and there was a pleasant scent of pine trees.

"I think we're in the Mediterranean somewhere," Ibraheem said. "Maybe in Al Sham. Our shadows are pointing away from the sun so south must be there."

He pointed in a direction that led away from the road. "That means we can either walk southeast or north-west. I say we go southeast. That way we'll get to Al-Quds if we're in Al Sham," Ibraheem said.

It was a shrewd assessment of the situation and as things turned out Ibraheem was right.

The children agreed to follow his lead and set off towards Al-Quds. They had walked for more than an hour when they saw a sharp bend in the road ahead of them. There were some trees growing near the road which led across a small river. As they came closer, they heard shouting and yelling and someone calling for help. The three children rushed forward. When they came around the bend, they saw a horse cart. Around it several men were fighting. Two men were protecting the cart while three were attacking them. Another five men lay dead on the road. From inside the cart a girl's voice was calling out "Help! Bandits are attacking us! Help!"

By the time our three heroes reached the scene two more bandits and a defender were dead and the last of the men defending the cart was badly wounded. Only a few more moments and the bandit would kill him too. The children ran forward, grabbed weapons that were lying on the road and attacked the bandit. Now the tables were turned!

"Here, take this you dirty villain!" Menalik shouted as he struck the bandit.

"And this and this!" Ibraheem and Zaria cried out.

The bandit was unable to fight against so many and in no time at all they had defeated him. Sadly, the last man defending the cart also sank to the ground. He was mortally wounded.

"Save her," he said and died.

Ibraheem pulled aside the canvas that covered the opening of the cart and looked in. He ducked away quickly because the girl in it threw a pot at him. The pot fell onto the road with a loud clanging sound.

The girl buried her face in her hands and began to cry.

Zaria climbed into the cart and put her arm around the girl's shoulders to console her.

"It's all right," Zaria said. "It's over now. The bandits are all dead. We'll help you."

The girl looked at her in surprise.

"You mean you're not with the bandits?"

"Certainly not," Ibraheem said. "We were walking along the road when we heard you calling for help so we came and helped to defeat the bandits."

"What's your name?" Menalik asked.

The girl looked at him and wiped her tears.

"My name's Adina. Help me get back to Al-Quds and my father will reward you handsomely."

"So, this is the road to Al-Quds," Ibraheem said triumphantly. "I knew it."

Adina looked at him strangely.

"Of course, this is the road to Al-Quds. Where else would it go? You really didn't know what road you're travelling on?"

"I think we'll explain it later," Zaria said quickly. "For now, I think it's better if we leave this place as fast as we can. Who knows if there are more bandits in the woods here"?

That was one thing they all agreed on so Ibraheem and Menalik sat at the front and somehow managed to get the horse going while Zaria spent time in the back getting to know Adina better.

Sitting on a horse drawn cart was much better than walking and the children, whose feet were a bit sore already, were glad they had met Adina. The cart rumbled along the Kevish Ridge towards Al-Quds. 'Kevish' is the Hebrew word for road, so they were on Ridge Road, which leads from Bethel to Al-Quds. As they got nearer to the capital of the Al Sham Empire the road became busier. They were relieved not to be travelling alone anymore and when they encountered some soldiers

Adina informed them about the attack on her cart. A group of soldiers quickly set off to investigate. At last, the greatest city on earth came into view and after they passed the town gate Adina directed the boys to her home through the bustling noisy streets. It was sunset by the time they stopped outside a huge villa.

The Sho'er, as a doorman is called in Hebrew, opened the huge wooden front door. As soon as Adina told him about the attack a hue and cry was raised over the mansion. Adina's parents came running and were overjoyed to find their beloved daughter unhurt.

"They saved me," Adina said as she pointed to her new friends. "Without them the bandits would have taken me, but my friends arrived just in time and defeated the bandits in a fierce fight."

Her father, Hiram Baal, walked down the steps to our three heroes.

"You have saved my only daughter, my light and joy in this world. From now on, my family shall be your family and my home shall be your home. I am Hiram Abibaal Baal, member of the senate and friend of Sulaimān Ibn Dāwūd (A). All Al-Quds is open to you, my friends."

Zaria prodded Ibraheem with her elbow and whispered in his ear "See, I told you this would be a Kubwa adventure!"

That evening there was a great rejoicing in the senator's villa and they all ate and drank happily, the senator and his family because Adina had been saved and our three heroes because their fortunes had reversed dramatically. Instead of being homeless vagrants on an unknown road they now were members of one of the most important families in Al-Quds.

5

Chapter 2

The children spent several wonderful days in Al-Quds. Adina was delighted to show her new friends around the holy city. They watched a chariot race at the Circus Maximus and they even got to see Sulaimān Ibn Dāwūd (A) during a meeting of the senate. Hiram Baal introduced them to Sulaimān (A) on his way in and the great man gave them a smile and a nod as a sign of recognition.

It was summer and the heat in the city was stifling. After leaving the senate, they stood in front of the building not knowing what to do.

"It's too hot to walk about the city," Ibraheem said.

"Have you forgotten Zazzau already?" Zaria teased him.

"I wish we could have some fun in the water," Menalik replied.

"One of my uncles has a large pool at his estate," Adina told them. "It's not far from Al-Quds. If we take the cart we can be there in an hour."

They all thought it was a good idea and a bit later that day they cart drew up at the estate in question. Adina's uncle was in Al-Quds, but the slaves on the estate knew her well and were only too happy to allow the children access to the pool.

It was a large pool, shallow at one end and then gradually sloping down towards the middle where it suddenly became deeper. They jumped into the shallow water where they could all stand, and happily splashed about.

"This is fantastic!" Menalik grinned. "Why didn't we come here before?"

He dashed water at Ibraheem.

After splashing around for a while Ibraheem challenged the others.

"I race you to the far side," he said and began to swim.

Menalik and Zaria tried their best to overtake him, but it was no good. Ibraheem reached the other end of the pool first and shouted happily "I'm the winner!"

It was only when Zaria and Menalik reached him that the children noticed Adina hadn't joined them. She was still at the other end of the pool and didn't look very happy.

"Adina!" Zaria called. "What's the matter?"

"I can't swim," Adina replied.

The children quickly went back to Adina.

"Come on, Adina," Zaria said. "I'll teach you how to swim. It's not difficult."

While the boys were splashing about, Zaria showed Adina how to move her arms and legs properly. The boys were getting quite wild at the shallow end of the pool and water often splashed in Adina's face, so the girls began to move towards the middle of the pool.

There was a long hedge at one end of the pool. On the other side one of the household slaves was trying to ride in a wild horse. It was a beautiful brown horse from far away Arabia that Adina's uncle had bought the night before. It was also a very wild and stubborn creature that had so far defied any attempts to ride it.

On this particular occasion the slave, a strong man with piercing eyes and braided hair called Sanad, tied the horse to a wooden post and then jumped on it from behind. The horse reared up in panic and tore the rope from the post. The slave still clung to its neck. The horse kicked violently and then leapt forward across the hedge. The slave was thrown off and the horse landed on the tiled floor around the pool. It skidded on the tiles and fell into the water somewhere between the boys and the girls.

The horse thrashed wildly in the water and made a horrible noise. It was a frightening spectacle. The boys climbed out of the pool to safety. The swimming lesson was forgotten. Zaria stared at the wild horse in horror while Adina backed away from it.

Adina didn't realize she was getting into deeper water and she forgot all about the sudden drop in the middle of the pool. Another step backwards and another step and Adina lost her footing. She slipped under water. When her head went under, she bumped her head on one of the steps. She forgot everything Zaria had told her. Adina thrashed her arms in panic and when she couldn't get her head out of the water she screamed for help. Nobody heard her.

The horse slowly managed to get to shallower water where it climbed out of the pool. It had calmed down again and let the slave take hold of the rope round its neck.

Ibraheem and Menalik watched the slave as he tried to pull the wet horse away from the pool. Only then did Zaria remember Adina. She turned round, but couldn't see her friend anywhere.

"Adina!" She called wondering where she had gone so quickly. She called louder and attracted the attention of the boys and the slave. Ibraheem walked over.

"She's down there!" He yelled and pointed to the deep water.

Zaria quickly dived and pulled Adina up to the surface while Ibraheem jumped into the water to help her. All the noise and shouting attracted more slaves from the house who came out to see what was the matter. Adina was pulled from the water. She didn't move. Menalik and Ibraheem quickly rolled her onto her side to help her breathe. They opened her mouth and pushed her chest. Some water came from her mouth, but she didn't wake up.

"Send for the roof," someone said. A roof is what doctors were called in ancient Al-Quds. Sanad rushed to get another horse and rode for the nearest roof. They only came back an hour later.

All this time the children were shaking in fear and horror. Adina, their friend was dead. Her father had trusted them with his daughter's life, had taken them into his home and his family, and now she was dead. It was an unimaginable nightmare.

The roof just took one look at Adina and shook his head.

"She is breathing, but I can't wake her up," he said sadly. "She needs a priest."

Just then Adina's uncle came back. He rushed to the poolside where he found his niece.

"By the immortal Yahweh!" He cried. "What evil has befallen her?"

When he had heard everything, he started yelling.

"You will be crucified!" He shouted at Sanad. "And your horrible children will be thrown to the lions! Just you wait till Adina's father hears about this!"

He rushed off in anger and sent messages to Adina's father and to the Mishtarah who are the police in Al-Quds.

Chapter 3

The three children were crying bitterly. Sanad merely stood in silence with his head bowed. He, who had once been a mighty and respected warrior, to be crucified, to die on the cross like so many other criminals in the Al Sham Empire! The shame was unbearable.

The slaves picked up Adina's body and carried her into the house. Only one man stayed behind. He was a middle-aged man. His hair and eyes were dark and he had a large beard. With sadness in his eyes, he looked on as Adina was carried away. His name was Bagayogo. He was a Timbuktu slave who worked as a teacher in the household. It was his job to educate Adina's three cousins and he also knew Adina well as she was a frequent guest. He turned to Sanad and the three children.

"Redemption," he said sternly. "Redemption is the only course open to you now, unless that is, of course, you want to die a most horrible death."

"What do you mean?" Ibraheem asked. "What is 'redemption'?"

Bagayogo frowned. "Redemption means that you redeem yourselves. You must pay for what you have done and buy back your freedom and your life."

They looked confused.

"Are you also talking about Al Sham punishment?" Sanad asked acidly.

"No," Bagayogo said gently. "What I mean is that you have to undo what happened here today. Only you can make this happen and if you don't want to die a terrible death, then I suggest you follow me and do as I tell you to."

"I still don't understand," Sanad said, "but whatever he's talking about can't be worse than dying on a spike or," he looked at the children, "being torn to pieces by lions."

He followed Bagayogo.

"Unless anyone's got a better idea," Menalik said, "we should go with him."

Their hearts heavy with sorrow and their knees weak with fear the children quickly ran after the Timbuktu slave.

"No time to be lost now," Bagayogo called out. "Quick Sanad! Get the five best horses and come round to the front."

While Sanad dashed for the horses the children helped the Timbuktu slave to gather some things from the house. Most importantly, he took a bag of gold coins from the master's office.

"Don't do this, Bagayogo!" Some of the other slaves said. "You know what happens to runaway slaves. You'll end up on a spike like Sanad or even worse!"

But the harsh and inhumane punishments he would have to face if the authorities caught them didn't deter Bagayogo. He knew what he had to do. Others might think he was helping fugitives from the law, but he knew better.

Within minutes they ran out of the building and found Sanad waiting with the horses. They mounted them and rode off at top speed.

"To Eilat!" Bagayogo shouted. "Our only hope is to catch a ship bound for Asmara."

They knew that they had a head start of an hour at the most, then the Mishtarah would come to arrest them.

When the Mishtarah arrived at the villa and discovered the criminals had fled, they sent out messages in different directions to alert troops all over Al Sham to be on the lookout for two runaway slaves and three children who had murdered an Al Sham citizen.

Then they arrested all the slaves in the villa. Under Al Sham law, all slaves in a household were put to death if one of them killed their master. It was not clear if the law applied as Adina had not really been dead, but the Mishtarah decided to leave the matter for a court to decide. Their heads bowed and some of them crying, the slaves were taken away in chains while Adina's body was placed in a carriage and returned to her parents' estate.

One of the messengers sent by the Mishtarah took the road to Eilat. Thanks to the efficient Al Sham stage post system the rider could change horses at regular intervals so that he always had a fresh horse to ride. By the time the fugitives arrived in Eilat the messenger was forty minutes away from the port.

Against regulations Bagayogo rode straight onto the docks where many ships from across the Empire lay moored.

"Transport to Asmara," he called as they rode past ships. "We seek transport to Asmara."

"We are Asmara bound," a short, stocky man said in Timbuktu.

"We need immediate passage," Bagayogo said. Have you got room for five passengers? We'll pay you well."

The man looked at each member of the exhausted party. They were dusty and sweaty and had obviously ridden hard.

"We sail this evening," he said, "to Tio."

"Sail now," Bagayogo said, "and we'll pay you double."

The man looked at them critically.

"I don't want no trouble with the law," he said.

"You can have the horses too," Sanad said.

"But we must depart at once," Bagayogo urged. "To Djibouti."

"Djibouti?" The man said in surprise.

"Here, open your hand," Bagayogo said and gave the man a handful of gold coins. It was enough to hire the entire ship.

The man greedily eyed the bag from which Bagayogo had taken the coins.

"Step right aboard," he said. "We sail at once."

The ship with our fugitives on board cleared the port at the very moment when the messenger from the Mishtarah arrived with an urgent order for the port master to be on the lookout and detain two slaves accompanied by three children.

The quadriremes sped out of the port pushed forward by two rows of oars. Out at sea a pleasant breeze came up and the vessel gathered speed in a southerly direction. For the first time since Adina's death, they had nothing to do and were able to sit quietly.

"Now then," Sanad said, "not that I'm ungrateful for getting away from Al Sham justice, or should I say retribution, but what are we doing here and where is Djibouti?"

Bagayogo smiled.

"Ah," he said, "so many questions in one. "Where shall I start…?"

"Just start at the beginning," Menalik said.

"Quite right, my young friend," Bagayogo chuckled. "The problem is, sometimes there's more than one beginning, it all depends on our perspective and the questions we face, but let me see… the simple answer would be that we must hasten to the Djibouti with all possible speed."

"So, what is in Djibouti?" Zaria asked impatiently.

"Djibouti," Bagayogo said, "is where the entrance to the underworld lies. It is the one place where the Jassasah descend into the underworld and the only place where the flower of life grows."

"Jassasah!? Flower of life!? What are you talking about?" Zaria asked.

"Jassasah is big hairy being or creature created by Allah (SWT)," Ibraheem said.

"Everything is created by Allah (SWT). You mean a gorilla?" She asked

"No, it is a special creature that is rarely seen by humans, but it can speak like us." He answered.

"If its rarely seen by humans, have you guys seen one? Asked Zaria

"No"

"How do you know so much about Jassasah"

"I read the Jassasah Hadith"

"Wait there is a Jassasah Hadith did Rasulullah see him? Tell me what happened?"

"No Rasulullah (S) didn't see him one of the Sahaba saw him with the Dajjal. I will tell you all about it later"

"A Timbuktu fairy tale," Sanad said disparagingly.

"Is it true?" Menalik asked. "Can people really go down to the underworld and bring back this special flower?"

"By Yahweh this can't be true," Sanad said.

"And yet it has been done before," Bagayogo replied. He looked across the sea where the coastline had receded into the distance. The sea was calm and the fresh sea air filled his lungs.

"A long, long time ago," Bagayogo began, "there was a man called Memnon. He was the son of King Tithonus of Ethiopia and renowned across the world as the best warrior and poet of his time. It is said that his music and singing could charm the birds, fish and wild beasts, coax the trees and rocks into dance, and divert the course of rivers.

He was a hero of old who saved the great city state of Nok. For when their ship came close to the bewitching singing of the sirens, Memnon drew his endongo and played music that was louder and more beautiful, drowning out the Sirens' bewitching songs.

But the deed he is most famous for concerns his wife Barsine. On the day of her wedding, Barsine was attacked by a Jinn. In her efforts to escape the Jinn, Barsine fell into a nest of vipers and suffered a fatal bite on her heel.

Her body was discovered by Memnon, who, overcome with grief, played such sad and mournful songs that all the jinn, Angels and Yahweh wept. On their advice, Memnon travelled to the underworld and by his music softened the heart of the king of Jassasah (he was the only person ever to do so), who agreed to allow Memnon to return with him to earth with the flower of life on one condition: he should walk in front of him and not look back until they both had reached the upper world.

He set off with the Jassasah following, and, in his anxiety, as soon as he reached the upper world, he turned to look at him, forgetting that they both needed to be in the upper world. The Jassasah along with the flower vanished for the second time, but now forever."

Jassasah takes the flower of life back to the underworld.

Bagayogo looked at his travel companions.

"So, you see," he said, "it is possible to venture into the underworld and come out alive again. It is possible to save a loved one, if we follow the instructions of Jassasah."

Zaria clapped her hands in excitement.

"Now that's what I call a Kubwa adventure," she said, feeling much better again at the prospect of saving Adina.

"A Kubwa adventure?" Bagayogo frowned disapprovingly. "It is not a matter to be taken lightly," he warned.

"So, let's say we're able to travel into the underworld," Ibraheem said, "how are we to soften the heart of Jassasah? We can't sing like Memnon."

They all looked at Bagayogo.

"Ah, yes," he said, "that is a problem. We'll just have to try and think of something."

"Try and think of something?" Sanad said incredulously. "You mean you want us all to go into the underworld, but you don't know how to get us out again?"

He looked angrily at Bagayogo.

"I can think of something much better. Let's pay the captain to sail past Asmara and go far north where the free tribes live who have not been enslaved by Al-Quds. There we'll be safe."

"But what about Adina?" Menalik said. "We've got to save her."

"Says who?" Sanad replied. "People die every day and we too will go to the afterlife soon enough. No need to hasten things."

"I say we must save her," Zaria said, "because she's our friend and because we owe her. I owe her because I was with her in the water and didn't see her slip, the boys owe her because they were too distracted by the horse to look for us girls, and you, Sanad, owe her because it was your horse that caused the tragedy."

"I suppose you have a reason why Bagayogo owes her as well?" Sanad said sarcastically.

Zaria shook her head.

"Why are you doing all this?" Ibraheem asked.

"A famous man once said 'If my body is enslaved, my mind is still free'. And it is so with me. I was made a slave, but my mind is still free. My mind sees a young girl whose life is cut short and several of her friends who must suffer terribly for this. And my mind sees you too, Sanad, taken from your home, enslaved and now in danger of your life. So, what did my mind tell me? It told me to do what is right, to help those in need of help when it is in my power to do so."

The others looked down feeling a little embarrassed. Then Sanad raised his eyes to Bagayogo.

"I don't know if you're the bravest man I've ever met, or the most foolish, but beside you I'm shamed into looking like a coward. I'll follow you wherever you go and if it means doing battle in the shadowy lands of the underworld, then so be it!"

The children jumped up excitedly.

"You can rely on us," they said.

Chapter 4

The five friends spent the rest of the day and the evening talking about ways how they might deal with Jassasah once they were in the underworld, but none of them came up with any workable idea. They fell asleep late that night under the watchful and watching eyes of the ship's crew.

The next morning Menalik was the first to wake up. There was something unpleasant in his mouth and he had trouble breathing. He opened his eyes and tried to move his hands to his face to rub his eyes. He couldn't. Then he understood. His hands and feet were tied together and his mouth was gagged.

He looked around in horror and tried to scream, but the gag in his mouth only lets out a quiet sound. He turned his head to look for the others. Ibraheem was sleeping next to him. Menalik turned on his side and kicked Ibraheem with his two feet tied together. One by one the others woke up.

The ship's captain walked over to them. He kicked Bagayogo and laughed cruelly.

"Thank you for that bag of gold, old fool. The question is what to do with you now? Two slaves I'd just throw overboard, but what about those children? Will anyone pay a ransom for them, eh?"

He removed the gag from the mouth of Bagayogo and kicked him.

"So old man, what about ransom, eh?"

Bagayogo looked at his captor in distaste. What could he say? They were on the run from Al Sham justice. Far from anyone paying a ransom for them the Al Quds were more likely to pay the ship's crew for murdering them. There was nothing to say. He turned his face away and looked at the clear blue sky. A beautiful sky. Would it be the last time they could see it before they too had to descend into the dark underworld?

"So that's how it is," the evil captain said. "Well, well, no loss of mine." He shook the bag of gold coins in Bagayogo' face and laughed.

"Ship ho!" One of the sailors called.

The captain left the doomed prisoners and hurried to the foredeck. With everyone looking at the prisoners another ship had approached unseen. It was closing fast. The captain realized what kind of ship it was and stood petrified for a few moments.

"Pirates!" He shouted finally and gave some hurried orders. Men rushed to the oars and began to row furiously. The ship gained speed. Everyone watched the pirate ship with fear. They all knew that if the pirates caught up with them, they had no hope. For a while the pirate ship seemed to fall back, but then three rows of oars descended into the water and the pirate ship was propelled forward with force.

The five captives lay on deck helpless and unable to see what was going on. They could hear the ship's crew talking in fear about the pirates and wondered what would happen to them if the pirates did overpower their ship?

"The captain of our vessel already wants to kill us," Ibraheem thought, "so maybe it's good if the pirates catch us. Things can't get any worse at any rate."

Alas, how many times have people in a bad situation thought things couldn't get any worse?

The pirate ship closed fast and the crews of both vessels prepared for a fight. The pirates posted archers at the bow and started to shoot when they got in range. The first few arrows fell short, but then arrows began to hit the ship and the defending crewmen cowered behind wooden planks.

The captain yelled at the rowers put 'their backs into it', but then what did they care? They were slaves anyway.

The pirates got closer and the archers now had a clear shot of almost the whole ship. They changed tactics with devastating results. The next arrows that came flying left a thin, dark trail as they flew threw the air. Fire arrows! As soon as the first hit the sail it caught fire. The fire spread rapidly and without the force of the wind to push the ship forward it quickly lost speed in spite of the best efforts of the rowers.

The end came suddenly. The pirate ship caught up, a wooden boarding bridge came crashing down and the pirates rushed across. They were heavily armed and overpowered the crew in just a few minutes.

The deck was wet and slippery with red blood and men lay about crying in agony, the scene of all battles – a time of misery and pain where loved ones can never come home again.

The ship was on fire and could not be rescued anymore. The pirates ransacked the vessel and took everything of value. They also freed the slaves who were rowing below from their chains and untied our five heroes. With the hull burning fiercely they all went aboard the pirate ship.

The freed rowers stood separate from Ibraheem and his friends. The pirate captain, a tall strong man with dark hair, blazing eyes and a big beard looked at them.

"Men," he called to the rowers, "you were taken from your homes, put into chains and made to work until you die. I am Captain Erythraean. You are slaves no more! Join us, have your revenge on those who enslaved you! Join us and an equal share of everything we take from those who oppressed you!"

The freed slaves cheered.

Only one man was quiet. When the cheers subsided, he stepped forth.

"And if someone does not want to join you, Captain? What then?"

Captain Erythraean peered at him curiously. He himself had been a slave years ago, before he had managed to flee.

"The choice is yours," he said calmly. "We only want those of you with us who do so of their own free will. If you don't want to join us, you're free to go where you will the next time we get to shore."

The captain turned to our heroes.

"Well then, what have we here," he said. "Prisoners on board a trading ship."

The pirates had removed the gags from their mouths, yet their hands were still tied behind their backs.

"Sir," Ibraheem said politely, "we paid the captain of the ship a lot of money to take for us all-Hamam with all haste, but when we were sleeping his men bound us and robbed our gold."

"Gold, you say? Are you sure you're telling the truth?"

"What the boy says is quite true," Bagayogo said. He told the captain the amount they had paid for the journey and how many gold coins were still left in the bag.

The pirate captain looked angry and turned round. On the other side of the deck were the prisoners they had taken including the captain.

"Just minutes ago," Captain Erythraean said to the prisoners, "you told me you had no money, nothing of any value. And now I hear that there must be quite a lot of gold in your possession."

"And it's true," the fearless captain replied. "Everything we had went down with our ship."

"You liar!" Zaria shouted across the deck. "We all saw you put the bag of gold under your clothes just before we were attacked."

The captain went all red in the face and the pirates laughed.

"Search him," Captain Erythraean ordered.

Two of his men obeyed and moments later they pulled out a heavy bag. Captain Erythraean took it and looked inside.

"By the immortal Yahweh!" He said. "There's more gold in more here than we'd normally find on ten ships of this kind."

His men cheered loudly.

"So, you thought you could lie to me and deceive me?" He said to the captain who was whimpering and whining.

"Mercy," he pleaded. "Have mercy!"

"And what were you going to do with your passengers?" Captain Erythraean asked icily.

"Set them free," the captain replied.

"You said you would kill us all," Menalik shouted.

"Men!" Captain Erythraean called to his crew. "You've heard everything. This man took passengers on his ship who paid him well. Did he do his work? He robbed them and bound them and wanted to kill them. He had a ship full of slaves. He lied to me and tried to deceive me. He wanted to cheat you out of all this gold!"

He held the bag up high.

"What are we to do with him? Tell me your verdict!"

"Throw him overboard! Cut his throat! Death! Death!" The men shouted.

The terrified captain lay on the deck and began to cry loudly.

Captain Erythraean laughed.

"Now you cry, dog! Where was your mercy and your pity when you had the power?"

He pulled out a long sharp knife and walked to the weeping man."

"Please, Captain Erythraean!" Ibraheem said loudly. "Don't kill that man."

Captain Erythraean looked surprised.

"Why not? Did this man not want to kill you? What is he to you?"

Ibraheem looked at Captain Erythraean bravely.

"Because to kill someone like that, with his hands tied, would be murder. Maybe he was a murderer, but you are a better man than him."

Captain Erythraean walked to Ibraheem with his knife in his hand and gazed at him.

"So, you're saying if I kill that scoundrel now, you'd call me a murderer? Do you know what ship you're on?"

Ibraheem nodded.

"And still you plead for that man's life, that villain who would have murdered you if we had not come in time?"

Ibraheem swallowed hard. The shiny blade of the pirate's knife was close to his face. He looked Captain Erythraean in the eye.

"You're a free man, sir. I am standing here as your prisoner just as I was that man's prisoner. Enough people have died. Don't kill anymore, please."

Captain Erythraean looked at him thoughtfully.

"And if the Al Quds caught me, would you plead for my life as you're now pleading for his?"

Ibraheem nodded.

"By Hercules! Have you heard, my men? If this isn't the bravest boy I've ever met, then I don't know who is. And yet, we still have a problem. If I don't kill those villains, what am I to do with them? I can't let them go or they'd tell the Al Sham fleet about us."

"Let them row," Sanad said. "They forced slaves to row for them, now let them have what they did to others."

Captain Erythraean smiled. "And so, it shall be."

He gave an order and several of his men dragged the former captain and what was left of his crew down below deck where they were chained to wooden benches that were beside oars.

Up on deck, Captain Erythraean drew his knife again and went to Ibraheem. Ibraheem froze in fear and his shocked friends held their breath. Captain Erythraean grabbed Ibraheem by his shoulder, turned him round and cut the rope with which his hands were tied.

"Here," he said and gave Ibraheem his knife. "Take this and free your friends."

Chapter 5

Captain Erythraean was from the isles in the far south of the Al Sham Empire. From the day he was robbed of his home as a young boy, his life had been one filled with cruelty and hardship, yet at heart he was a kind man. He listened with sympathy to the story Ibraheem and his friends had to tell. At last, he shook his head.

"Venture down into the underworld," he said in disbelief. He gazed at the distant horizon across the blue sea. "If ever there was a journey that needed courage, then this is it. And you five are willing to do this for the sake of one Al Sham girl?"

"We must do so," Zaria said. "She's, our friend."

Captain Erythraean jumped up. "Do you hear that, my men? A girl who has the courage to face Jassasah himself. Are we to be put to shame by a girl?"

"Let's help them!" His men roared back.

"Set sail for Djibouti!" Captain Erythraean ordered.

The pirates proved to be far less ferocious and cruel than expected and during the two days it took them to reach Djibouti they came close to making friends.

On the last evening before reaching their destination, Captain Erythraean invited them for dinner in his cabin. They ate and drank in silence.

"Tomorrow, before sunrise," Captain Erythraean said, "we'll be at the

Djibouti." He paused and took a deep breath. "Then will be the time to say farewell, for you must go your way as we must go on our way. But there's one thing I want to do for you before we part."

He snipped his fingers and one of his men brought in a wooden box which he carefully placed in front of Captain Erythraean.

They all looked at the box with curiosity. A gift from a pirate captain was the last thing they had expected.

The captain lifted the lid and took out an instrument. It was a beautiful endongo with a gold frame and shiny silver strings.

The magic endongo

They all made big eyes and Captain Erythraean smiled at their wonder.

"Yes," he said, "it is stunningly beautiful, isn't it?"

"And you're really giving this to us?" Menalik said in disbelief.

"It must be worth a fortune," Ibraheem said.

"No, not a fortune," Captain Erythraean said. "It's priceless. The true value of this instrument is not so much what it's made of, but what it is."

"What do you mean?" Bagayogo asked.

This is the very same endongo that Memnon once played when he enchanted Jassasah with his mesmerizing music. It is a magic endongo."

He handed it to Bagayogo who inspected the instrument carefully. He was about to pluck a string, but Captain Erythraean quickly stayed his hand.

"Only play it when you really need it. You can only use it once."

"Why?" Menalik asked.

The captain laughed. Only a child would ask 'why'.

"It's the magic that was given to this marvelous instrument. It grants its owner, but one time the pleasure of hearing it. And now," he said, turning to Bagayogo, "it is yours."

Bagayogo bowed in gratitude.

"Thank you, Captain Erythraean. It is most generous of you. Your heart is in the right place. May I offer your heart a gift in return?"

"A gift from my heart?"

Bagayogo nodded.

"When we were first on your ship you freed the slaves and offered them the chance to take revenge."

"That's right," Captain Erythraean said. He suddenly had a hard, stony look in his eyes, the look of a man hardened by years of suffering.

"A wise man once said, 'All of a man's affairs become diseased when he wants to cure evils by evils. The more you seek revenge, Captain Erythraean, the more you fight and kill those who you think wronged you, the bitterer your heart will become until it is all eaten up by hatred. You will never find happiness like this, only bitterness."

"Then what is your gift for me?"

"Only this. Learn to let go. You cannot change what happened many years ago. Take your ship and sail away while you still can, far away to a distant land where you can live in peace, where you can find love and true happiness."

No one said anything for a while wondering how Captain Erythraean would respond. It is not every day that a pirate captain is asked to sail away and find a life of peace and love.

"Who said that?" He asked after a while.

Bagayogo looked confused.

"About my affairs becoming diseased if I cure evils by evils. Who said that?"

"Akhenaten, his name was Akhenaten. He was a Pharaoh visionary."

"I see," Captain Erythraean said. He looked at the children. "And what do you think, my young friends? You already saved the life of the man who wanted to murder you. What do you think I should do?"

Ibraheem thought for a moment.

"I think you should find happiness. We only live once. Why waste your life in hatred and bitterness if you are free to go somewhere where you can be happy?"

"So simple," Captain Erythraean said in disbelief. "Can it really be so simple? And yet, maybe you're right."

Captain Erythraean thought of the years he had spent fighting, robbing traders and killing men. The more he sought revenge, the more his hatred grew and yet he never seemed to find the one thing he wanted most: to forget the day slave traders murdered his parents and took him captive, to find peace in his heart.

He looked from Ibraheem to Bagayogo and said "Maybe your words are the best gift I've ever received. You're right. My heart was poisoned by seeking revenge. When I have taken you to the Djibouti we'll sail to distant shores in pursuit of happiness.

Chapter 6

Al-Quds, at the villa of Adina's father Hiram Abibaal Baal and her mother Tamar.

Adina lay on her death bed. She was wearing a Black dress and there was a wreath of flowers around her head. Her father placed a silver coin in her mouth, then her mother kissed her one last time and closed her eyes. All her family was gathered around the bed. Some were crying quietly, others wept without restraint.

Six bearers entered. They took position on both sides of the death bed, then lifted it onto their shoulders. Adina was carried out feet first. When she crossed to the front door a group of musicians began playing the most mournful, sad melody. They led the way through the busy streets of Al-Quds while Adina's family walked behind. When they crossed the city's sacred boundary the sides of the road were lined with wailing women who cried and wept and tore their clothing and hair in sadness and despair.

Adina's last journey was over soon. They reached the priest temple that would be her last resting place before going to her tomb.

Her father held a short speech remembering her life. At the end there was a brief silence, after which her family chanted a holy prayer. Her father and mother gazed upon the sweet face of their daughter, their only child, one last time.

The very next day Senator Hiram Abibaal Baal joined Sulaimān Ibn Dāwūd (A) and some 4000 soldiers. They marched from Al-Quds to Eilat where they boarded transport ships. Their destination: Saba.

Full of bitterness Senator Baal watched the shoreline recede. He knew the killers of his child had gone this way and he was determined to find them and have his revenge.

Chapter 7

A sailor rowed them ashore near the caves of Djibouti the next morning. Bagayogo clutched the magic endongo and a bag of silver coins, while the others carried food and drink and some other important things. From the little cove where they landed, they walked along a narrow path that led upwards. After a few minutes of hard climbing up the steep path they came out into the open. Below them the beautiful blue waters of the Mediterranean Sea stretched all the way to the horizon, and in that vast expanse the pirate ship sailed towards the west with all its sails hoisted.

Captain Erythraean had made up his mind to turn a new leaf in his life and go in search of peace and happiness far beyond the reach of the Al Sham Empire. Much to his own surprise most of his men had proved very willing to accompany him.

Our heroes gazed down at the ship and waved farewell. They saw a little figure wave back.

"Oh, I do hope Captain Erythraean finds a new home for himself," Zaria said.

"Who knows?" Sanad replied pessimistically. His own experience in life had taught him not to expect anything good.

"To the temple, then," Ibraheem said.

There was a temple built above the entrance to the caves that led to the underworld and Bagayogo insisted that they go and make a sacrifice to the Yahweh before attempting to enter the underworld.

"We must show our humility to the Yahweh," Bagayogo said, "or we are doomed before we even begin our journey."

The temple was a curious round building, quite different from any other temple they had ever seen. They passed through the entrance into the dark, smoke-filled interior. The outside world was shut out and an eerie silence pervaded the hall. They stopped and looked about in awe.

"Strange," Menalik said. "I can hear whispers."

They all strained their ears, and it was true. There was the sound of many people whispering, yet when they looked about, they couldn't see anyone.

"Let's not waste time," Ibraheem said.

Bagayogo nodded and approached the altar. He placed several coins in the appointed place and lit some incense. The aromatic smoke rose up and added its scent to the smoke in the hall. Bagayogo said a prayer to the immortal Yahweh and then they sang a short holy song together.

They were all happy when they could leave the temple again.

"What a weird place," Zaria said.

"Where we're heading now will be a thousand times stranger and scarier," Bagayogo said. "Make your peace with the Yahweh and the world, my friends, then follow me."

From the temple, it was a few minutes' walk down to the shore where the entrance to the underworld lay. Several men and women knelt around the entrance, praying for their loved ones who had entered the underworld. A priest dressed all in white accepted their offerings and gave his blessings. Behind him was the dark opening to the underworld from which white and yellow fumes emerged. Not even the Hebrew priests had the ability to enter the cave and come out alive. Bagayogo gave the priest an offering and asked him to pray for him and his companions.

"But you won't return alive," the surprised priest protested.

Our heroes ignored him and walked towards the dark cave. Sanad carried some torches which they lit before entering the dreaded opening to a world no one wanted to cross. The air was filled with suffocating fumes and they found it almost impossible to breathe.

They hurried along through the narrow dark space that led down deep into the earth. As they descended deeper and deeper into the rocky darkness, they struggled to get their breath until they were forced to tie cloths soaked in water in front of their mouths. Then, quite suddenly everything changed. The narrow space of the passage opened up into a large area and the suffocating fumes cleared and they were able to inhale clear cool air again. They stood on the bank of a river! It extended from one side to the other and the light of their torches was lost in the distance.

"The River Malve," Bagayogo said gravely.

"What is it?" Menalik asked.

"It's the river of woe," Bagayogo said, "we have to cross it to reach the underworld. It is here that we'll need the silver coins we brought along."

"Look!" Zaria said. "There are people moving along the river bank."

"They're not humans, they are jinn waiting for Marid," Bagayogo said sadly. "He's the ferryman who takes the Jinn across the river, but only those who have a silver coin to pay him are taken."

"So, what happens to the others?" Menalik asked.

"They're stuck here forever," Bagayogo replied. "They can't go back to the world of the living and they can't get across the River Malve to the underworld."

"I don't like this place," Sanad said. "Let's do what we have to do and get it over with as fast as possible."

"Quite right, Sanad," Bagayogo said and walked towards the river.

When they reached the riverbank the envious shadows of the Jinn moved aside to let them pass through. Marid the ferryman was waiting. He looked at them critically. He wore a dark cloak and a hood was pulled over his head. His face was hidden in the dark, only his eyes emitted a faint red glow.

"Why are you coming here?" His gloomy voice whispered and echoed through the cavernous space. "I cannot take you."

Bagayogo gave each of his companions a silver coin.

"Accept your fare and do your duty, O Marid!" He said in a commanding tone. He put a coin in Marid's hand and pushed past him to board the ferry. The others did the same.

Marid looked angrily at them, but then shrugged his shoulders.

"Beware of what you wish for!" He warned them.

"We've got no time to waste," Ibraheem urged him.

"So be it," Marid said and steered them across the Malve.

Ibraheem held his torch over the water and looked down.

"That's strange," he said. "There's no reflection in the water, it's totally black."

"Reflection?" Marid chuckled darkly. "What reflection can there be from the waters of woe?"

Marid set them off at the other side of the river. There was a worn path, trodden by millions of weary feet that led the way from the shore. Ibraheem eagerly strode out, but stopped after a short distance. In front of him was a huge, intimidating gate.

"The Adamantine Gate," Bagayogo said.

"What's adamantine?" Menalik asked.

"That means it's harder and stronger than anything else in the world and," he sighed, "it's guarded by Rompo."

"Isn't Rompo a three headed dog?" Ibraheem asked.

"That's right," Bagayogo said. "He admits the dead into the underworld, but he lets no one out again."

"Great," Sanad said sarcastically. "So, what about us?"

Ibraheem walked up to the gate and knocked.

There was a hollow clanging sound and then the gate slowly rumbled open. Rompo glared at them with his fiery eyes, but let them pass unharmed.

"That was easy," Menalik said.

"Sure," Sanad replied, "we're going in."

Immediately after the gate, they were confronted by three judges whose job it was to judge the Jinn and send them to different parts of the underworld. It was impossible to pass them without judgement. Ibraheem tried to walk past, but his legs were frozen to the ground. The judges looked severely at our five heroes. They consulted their books and talked to each other.

"You're not in our books," they finally said fiercely.

"We demand to see Jassasah!" Ibraheem said.

"Jassasah, King Jassasah," they whispered, "ruler of the shadowy land of the Jinn, Lord of the underworld. You're not in our books and we cannot judge you. So be it. Be on your way to King Jassasah!"

They walked through the shadowy land. Their blazing torches were the only bright light and all around the dead looked at them with envy. It was a gloomy, dark place. Black mists swirled above them, shadowy figures gazed at the living and all about there were whispers that told of lives and joys gone by.

Then they stood before Jassasah. He sat upon a throne so dark that even the light of their torches could not make it visible.

"What are you doing here?" Jassasah growled at them. "You do not belong here. This is no place for the living."

"We have come for the flower of life for our friend Adina," Ibraheem said boldly and stepped up to King Jassasah.

"The calendula," Jassasah said gravely, "belong to my realm. They are not for you."

"We have brought a gift," Bagayogo said quickly.

"A gift? What gift could any mortal give me?"

"The most beautiful music you have ever heard, King Jassasah," Ibraheem said.

Jassasah was intrigued.

Jassasah, King of the Underworld

"What?" He said. "More beautiful, even than the music Memnon played for me?"

"For you to judge, your majesty," Menalik said. "We only ask that calendula is here to listen as well."

Jassasah chuckled.

"And then, I suppose, you want to take calendula and escape to the land of the living while I'm listening to your beautiful music?" He said and laughed.

"Memnon once tricked me in this way and almost managed to take one of the plants back to the land of the living. Do you really think I'll be so foolish to let it happen a second time?"

"Your majesty," Zaria quickly said, "we know it's not possible to deceive you. All we want is to play some music for you. We have come over a long way and we beg you humbly to grant our request."

"Indeed," Jassasah said, "you have come over a long way, though how you want to make your way back I cannot imagine, past Rompo and the ferry that only takes its passengers one way."

He laughed cruelly.

Bagayogo took out the magic endongo. It sparkled and shone brightly in the dark realm of Jassasah, brighter even than the fires of the blazing torches. Jassasah looked at it with interest.

"Very well," he said at last and had calendula sent for.

When calendula was brought before them, the plant looked at them with sad mournful eyes. She tried to speak to them, but the sounds coming from her mouth were mere whispers about life., but she was unable to say what she really wanted.

Bagayogo let his fingers glide across the strings of the magic endongo. The most beautiful music ever filled the air. When Memnon had played the instrument, it had been his skill that enchanted Jassasah, but now the endongo was filled with the sound of divine love and friendship. The enchanting music filled the air. All the Jinn and even King Jassasah stared at the magic endongo and listened to its wonderful tune.

Ibraheem dashed forward and grabbed a calendula plank.

"Let's go," he said.

He ran away and the others quickly followed him.

"Remember!" Bagayogo shouted, "you mustn't look back. Whatever you do, don't look back!"

They ran through the milling crowds of the Jinn towards the Adamantine Gate. When they got near the gate mighty Rompo stood in their way and growled at them with his three heads.

Rompo

Ibrahim stopped dead in his tracks and held on to the calendula.

"Let us pass!" Ibraheem commanded.

"No one leaves the shadowy lands of Jassasah," Rompo snapped.

"We're not Jinn, or cryptids and we will leave," Sanad said and drew his sword. He jumped forward and slashed at Rompo. The three headed dog quickly pulled its head away and attacked Sanad with another head. Rompo bit the iron sword and his hellish teeth sliced through the metal like a hot knife through butter. Another one of his heads drew close to Sanad's face and growled "No one leaves!".

Then Menalik had an idea. He walked up to Rompo and patted the mighty dog's head.

"Good doggie," he said. "Let's play a game."

"A game?" Rompo said in surprise.

No one ever played games in the underworld. The idea of anyone patting him on the head and asking him, the ferocious guardian of the Adamantine Gate, to play a game was so daring, so unusual that Rompo was intrigued.

"A game?" Rompo repeated not sure if he had heard correctly. "What game?"

"It's very simple and lots of fun," Menalik said. He opened his bag. "Look here! I've got some nice balls to play with. Let's play fetch. I throw the balls and you fetch them. We'll have lots of fun together."

Rompo looked at Menalik in astonishment, then to the balls and back to Menalik again.

"Have fun?" He said in disbelief. How could anyone think of having fun in the underworld? And yet there it was: A boy who not only seemed to be totally unafraid of him, but who also wanted to play with him and have fun together. This had never happened before. Rompo thought hard about the things his master, King Jassasah, had forbidden him to do, but could not remember Jassasah ever saying anything about playing games or having fun. He decided to give it a try.

"Very well, then. Let's play."

Menalik smiled at Rompo.

"Great," he said. "I love playing with dogs." He threw three balls in different directions and winked at Ibraheem.

Suddenly Ibraheem understood what Menalik was doing. When Rompo stretched his necks in different directions to reach the balls, Ibraheem quietly the calendula past the mighty dog and through the open gate. Much to his own surprise Rompo enjoyed playing fetch. He dropped the balls one by one in front of Menalik who threw them as far as he could, and each time another member of their group managed to sneak past Rompo until only Menalik was left.

When Rompo dropped another ball in front of Menalik he suddenly noticed that the others were missing. He looked around and spotted them on the far side of the Adamantine Gate running towards the River Malve. Rompo understood that Menalik had tricked him. He was furious. His three heads turned towards Menalik. Six angry eyes blazed in a fiery red at him and three mouths opened, revealing rows of hellish teeth. Menalik felt the dog's foul breath. He decided not to wait for Rompo to bite him. He threw the balls at Rompo' noses and ran away with all speed. Every step took him farther away from the gate and from his friends, but he had no choice.

Rompo was beside himself with rage. Tricked by a little boy! Balls thrown at his nose! It was too much. He ran after Menalik barking furiously. He saw the boy running through the shadowy crowds of the Jinn towards King Jassasah who was still entranced by the music of the magic endongo. Menalik had almost reached Jassasah when the music stopped.

King Jassasah looked up as if woken from a dream and looked around.

"Where are your friends?" He asked Menalik. Then he spotted Rompo.

"By the immortal Yahweh!" He cried and jumped up. "What are you doing here?"

There were crowds of the Jassasah creatures milling about. When they saw Rompo they immediately realized the opportunity. The Adamantine Gate was unguarded. There was a roar and the Jassasah creatures rushed towards the gate.

"Quick, you fool!" King Jassasah shouted at Rompo. "Back to the gate!"

It was a mad race between Rompo and the Jassasah creatures. Rompo understood how foolish he had been. What would the world of the living be like if the Jassasah creatures were allowed to escape from the underworld. He ran with all his might and main. He crashed through the throngs of the Jassasah creatures and then, with one last mighty jump, he landed in front of the gate and flung its doors shut with his hind legs while his three heads growled and snarled at the creatures. Rompo had arrived just in time. One second more and the creatures would have been through the gate.

Jassasah sat down in relief and mopped his brow.

"Phew," he said. "That was a narrow thing. Now, what was that silly dog doing here?" He looked at Menalik and said sternly "Something tells me it had something to do with you."

Chapter 8

Ibraheem, Zaria, Bagayogo and Sanad reached the River Malve. They turned round expecting to see Menalik come any minute. They waited and waited, but there was no Menalik. Ibraheem became desperate. It could not be that he got the calendula, but lost his brother.

"Wait here," he said to Adina. He ran back to the Adamantine Gate and came just in time to see it crashing shut. He banged his fists against the gate, he screamed, he cried, but it was no use. The gate stayed shut.

Heartbroken Ibraheem turned back to the river. What could he do? When he reached the others, he had tears in his eyes and told them what had happened.

"What about the challenge?" Zaria asked. "If we fulfil it, we'll get him out again, won't we?"

Ibraheem shook his head. "You challenged us to be on that boat together. Without Menalik we can't fulfil it."

"The gate must open again sooner or later," Bagayogo said. "The underworld can't keep out the Jinn. We'll just have to wait."

They went back to the Adamantine Gate and sat down to wait for as long as it would take. As time went by Marid brought more and more of the Jinn across the river. Fallen soldiers, old people, children of the Jinn of illness and many others milled about staring with wonder at the living and not understanding why the gate was closed.

Whispers filled the air and mingled with the echoes that bounced off the bare rock all around. There was nothing to say for Ibraheem and his friends. They sat in an eerie silence while the hours went by. Gradually the cool air thickened and death pervaded everything. Their eyes grew heavy and their breathing slowed. Those around them stopped moving about and stood to watch. Soon, they knew, they would all be together. And high up, far above the gate, an eye peered down. It was Rompo. Victory was almost his and he watched with a quiet sense of satisfaction. Had he not told them that no one ever left the underworld?

Ibraheem's gaze was fixed on his hands. His usually restless fingers were barely moving now. His skin became darker and the blood vessels stood out in purple.

"They're purple! How strange" His mind deep down told him. "Why should they be purple" They shouldn't be purple!" His mind kept nagging him. Yet he was too tired and drowsy to think. "Wake up! Wake up!" His mind told him. "Something's wrong! Quickly wake up!"

This last thought managed to get through to him and he moved his eyes. He suddenly realized that something was indeed wrong, terribly wrong. He wanted to stand up, but his arms and legs wouldn't move. A single tear ran down his face. He understood he was dying.

"I don't want to die!" He told himself again and again. The drowsiness was pulling him into the darkness. He struggled and he fought with all his might and main to wake up and get control over himself again. He was afraid. Then his heart began pumping harder. His blood flowed again. At last, his mouth opened, and he took a deep breath. He could move again! All around there were excited whispers and high up Rompo looked down in dismay.

Ibraheem forced himself to stand up and went to Zaria. He shook her and slapped her face until she, too, awoke. Then they saved Bagayogo and Sanad. When they understood how close they had been to death Zaria gave Ibraheem a big hug and kissed his cheek.

"You're my hero," she said.

"Indeed," Bagayogo said, "you saved us all."

Ibraheem blushed proudly.

"But now," Sanad said, "we have to leave."

"We can't leave Menalik behind," Ibraheem protested.

"We can't stay," Sanad replied. "Look at us all. Our veins are still dark, almost purple. If we don't leave now, we're never going to leave."

"If you fight and run away, you live to fight another day!" Bagayogo said. "We must go, Sanad is right, but we can try to return another time."

Ibraheem didn't want to go, but he knew they were right. His head hanging low he followed the others to the river. The calendula in his hand.

When they got to the River Malve the ferry had just arrived. The vessel emptied and they tried to board it. An angry Marid stood in their way and wouldn't let them pass.

"There's no way back," he snarled.

"Just take your fare and be quiet!" Ibraheem shouted.

Marid stuck his face into Ibraheem's.

"You would be angry with me?" He growled. "How dare you!"

"We're not leaving," Bagayogo said. "We were five when we came and we're still five, so you can take us."

"Trying to be clever with me?" Marid laughed. "What nonsense. You Africans always think you're so clever, but let me tell you something. Not one of you has ever left this place with all your cleverness."

This was turning out to be a serious problem. They eyed the river wondering if they could swim across. Marid saw where they were looking and laughed again.

"Want to go for a swim? Go ahead, just stick your finger into the water. The moment you touch it the river will carry you off forever."

Then Ibraheem had an idea.

"I'm sorry I was angry with you before, Marid. I just wanted to help you. It's a question of economics, you see."

Marid looked confused. No one had ever apologized to him before, let alone spoken of economics. The ferry was his business and over the millennia this was the first time anyone had shown an interest in it.

"Economics?" He said suspiciously. "What do you mean?"

"Well," Ibraheem began, "it's obvious that you're a good businessman. You charge everyone one silver coin for a trip across the river and you don't take any passengers who can't pay. Unfortunately, you're not using your ferry to capacity."

"Yes, I am," Marid protested. "Every time I make the crossing, I make sure the ferry is full."

"Really? Are you sure? So how come you go back to the other side all empty? If you take passengers both ways, you'll be able to earn a lot more. You might even double, your earnings."

Marid was astounded. He had never thought of this before and didn't know what to say.

"Of course," Ibraheem went on, "I know you're going to say that no one can leave here, and you're right. Look at those on the other side of the river who have no money to pay the fare, they're stuck there forever. So why not take passengers both ways as long as they can pay the fare? Take us, for example. We still have a bag full of silver so why not take us for a ride? It's not your concern, after all, where we are left at the end when our money is used up."

Marid was overwhelmed by the logic. It was true even those on the other side of the river couldn't return to the world of the living and it was equally true that he could earn more by taking passengers both ways.

"Why not," he said to himself. "All right then, pay the fare and I'll take you."

Each of them paid. When they were on board and the ferry moved across the river his friends patted Ibraheem on the back.

"Excellent thinking!" They said.

The rest was a piece of cake. Well, all right, not quite that easy. They had to walk up the narrow tunnels filled with horrible fumes and they had to remember not to look back, but they managed. To the surprise of everyone outside the entrance to the underworld suddenly two children and two men came out.

A priest who had seen them enter cried out in amazement.

"A miracle! They have returned from the realm of Jassasah. A miracle! Come, you must come with me!"

The priest quickly took them to the temple and told the high priest what had happened.

The high priest smiled at them in delight. A miracle at his temple meant thousands, no hundreds of thousands of visitors would come and make generous donations in the hope that they, too, would save a loved one. He quickly calculated how much more money he would earn and decided that he was going to be very rich in future.

"You must tell me everything," he said greedily.

Chapter 9

Menalik breathed a sigh of relief. Rompo had been hard on his heels and he'd barely escaped. He decided that King Jassasah might not be such a bad fellow after all. Ignoring the stern look, Menalik went to King Jassasah and climbed onto his lap. He put one arm around the king's neck and a hand on his chest and looked into the king's eyes.

"Thank you for helping me, King Jassasah," he said softly. "You're so nice, I like you."

King Jassasah was astounded. In all the thousands of years no one had ever said such a thing to him. He felt his heart melt and didn't know what to say.

"You know," Menalik went on, "I was playing with your dog and we were happy together, but then he got really angry with me." He looked up at King Jassasah with his charming little eyes. "But you're not angry with me, are you. You're such a nice man."

"You were playing with Rompo and you were happy?" King Jassasah said in disbelief.

Menalik nodded and explained the game of fetch to the king. Next, he happily talked about their adventures and how they'd come to be in the underworld. King Jassasah smiled a little and feeling encouraged Menalik was delighted to tell King Jassasah about their other adventures and how each challenge led to the new exciting and fun. King Jassasah listened in fascination. Mortals never came to him and told him their stories, they only hung about in silence feeling sorry for themselves.

"But tell me," King Jassasah said at last, "what did you do to make Rompo so angry?

"Oh, that," Menalik said and stuck his tongue against his cheek, but there was no way to avoid the question. He quickly told the truth and gave the king a big hug.

To his surprise King Jassasah laughed aloud.

"You little rascal," King Jassasah chuckled. "You actually managed to trick my guard dog to let your friends escape from my kingdom!" And with that he laughed again heartily. It was the first time in thousands of years that King Jassasah had laughed and he enjoyed it so much that he could not be angry with Menalik.

Menalik was still sitting on his lap when he suddenly burst into tears.

"But whatever is the matter?" Jassasah asked him.

Menalik looked at him with tears in his eyes. "I miss my mummy and daddy and now the gate is closed and Rompo is angry with me and won't let me out. Can you help me please?"

The king laughed again, he laughed so much that he cried.

"I don't know what to say about you and your brother and your friends," he laughed. "You tricked me with that magic endongo and you tricked Rompo and everything you do and tell me is so incredibly funny that no one in the world could possibly be angry with you."

King Jassasah snipped his fingers and a shadow appeared. He gave an order.

"Now don't you fret," king Jassasah said to Menalik. "All is well that ends well, and so it shall, if it has anything to do with me."

Menalik wasn't sure what the king meant, yet he felt that Jassasah was going to help. He gave Jassasah another big hug and kissed him on the cheek. King Jassasah went red in the face with embarrassment at this show of affection and patted Menalik on the back saying "Now, now, my little friend. Don't you worry."

Not long after there was a sound of wings fluttering through the air and a huge gryphon landed in front of King Jassasah. The gryphon looked at

Jassasah suspicious. Being summoned to the underworld was unheard of, yet the king had promised free passage and an order from the king was an order that had to be obeyed.

King Jassasah gave Menalik a hug and said "One piece of advice, my young friend, take care of what you do in life. You only have one life and whether it's long or short you'll always come here in the end. What I mean to say is, don't do anything foolish. Live a long and happy life and don't let anyone trick you into giving up your life. Life is meant to be lived, not thrown away. Can you promise me that?"

Menalik nodded. He didn't fully understand, yet he knew the king meant well.

King Jassasah gave the gryphon an order and then took Menalik's hands. "Time for you to leave this dreary place, my friend. The gryphon will fly you out and take you wherever you want to go in the world of the living."

"Thank you," Menalik said and climbed on the gryphon's back.

The king waved as the gryphon beat its wings and flew up.

"And remember!" The king shouted after him, "don't throw your life away! It's all you have."

The gryphon flew across the shadowy land. Menalik gazed down at all those poor souls who could never leave again and began to understand the king's warning. They flew across the Adamantine Gate. It was open again and the unhappy dead came streaming through it. Rompo spotted Menalik on the gryphon and looked up angrily, but there was nothing he could do and besides he was too busy guarding the gate.

The gryphon flashed through the passage to the world above and moments later emerged into the bright sunshine. Both Menalik and the gryphon breathed the fresh air happily and looked at the blue sky. Never had white clouds in a blue sky looked so beautiful before to Menalik. The warm sun made him treasure his life and he was determined to avoid going back to the underworld for as long as he ever could. He realized that the advice of King Jassasah was probably the best thing anyone could ever tell him.

"My friends," he called to the gryphon, "fly me to my friends!"

The mighty creature flew high up in the sky and peered down. When it found what it was looking for the gryphon dived down in a steep flight heading for the temple above the entrance to the underworld. In a trice they descended from the clouds to ground level and landed in front of the temple were astonished priests and pilgrims stared at them.

Ibraheem and the others were still sitting in the temple with the high priests when Menalik called out his name.

"Ibraheem!" The shout echoed through the temple. "Ibraheem where are you?"

Ignoring the priests Ibraheem jumped up and ran out of the building. When he spotted his brother on the gryphon he ran as fast as he could and took him in his arms. He squeezed Menalik tightly and gave his brother the biggest and mightiest hug ever. He understood that all the money the priest had talked about, indeed all the wealth in the world meant nothing compared with having his little brother back alive. Overcome with happiness the two brothers hugged each other closely while their friends, the priests and everyone else watched in amazement.

"A miracle!" One of the priests shouted.

"Let's get going!" Menalik said to his friends. "Just hop on."

They climbed onto the gryphon and flew up high into the beautiful blue sky. The wonderful fragrance of pine trees filled the air and below them the sound of waves on the shore made a heavenly sound. They were together again and they were all alive! It was the most wonderful feeling in the world.

Menalik laughed out loud as the wind blew through his hair.

"Fly, gryphon, fly," he shouted. "Fly us to Al Quds!"

The mighty creature obeyed and they shot through the sky.

Once they reached the priest temple in Al Quds Bagayogo took some of the flowers from the Calendula plant and prepared the tea. They all stood around Adina's body as Bagayogo put the tea to her lips. As the tea went down Adina's throat the swelling and inflammation on her brain immediately began to go down. After twenty minutes Adina regained conscientiousness and they told her all about their saga.

Soon after Adina went to see her mother. "My Baby! My Baby! You awake! Thank Elohim! Your awake!" Cried Tamar as she hugged and kissed Adina over and over again.

Adina told her mother everything, how she got hurt and how and how her new friends risked their lives to go to the ends of the earth to get the flower of life calendula and saved her.

"Go to your father, he is with Sulaimān Ibn Dāwūd (A) and the fleet in the red sea looking for you guys so that he will see that you are alive and tell him everything that you told me."

Chapter 10

After flying south-west for several hours, they approached the Al Sham fleet on its way to Saba. The gryphon puts his head down and they dived towards the warships and troop transports. When the gryphon was spotted panic broke out on the ships. There was shouting and the general alarm was sounded but the gryphon flew so fast that it landed on the deck of Sulaimān Ibn Dāwūd's (A) ship before any of the archers were ready. The children and their companions slid off the back of the gryphon in front of the amazed Al Quds. The huge bird flapped its wings and flew away again before anyone could say a word.

"By Elohim!" Sulaimān Ibn Dāwūd (A) exclaimed. "Who are you?"

Ibraheem and Menalik stood in front while Adina and Zaria were behind the two men.

"I can tell you who they are!" A voice boomed across the deck. "They're the murderers of my daughter!"

The angry voice belonged to Hiram Abibaal Baal.

"Have them put in irons, oh Sulaimān," he said.

Just then a little figure dashed out from behind Sanad and ran towards Senator Baal.

"Father! Father!" She cried and threw herself into his arms.

Senator Baal was overwhelmed and confused. He knew his daughter was dead and yet here she was in his arms; how could it be?

"There's obviously more to this than meets the eye," Sulaimān (A) said to Senator Baal. "Let's take them all below deck and hear what they have to say."

They told their adventures of the two powerful men who listened from beginning to end without saying a word.

"By Elohim!" Sulaimān (A) said again. "If this isn't the most incredible story I've ever heard, then I don't know what is. Such daring and bravery! I wish all my soldiers were just as brave and daring."

"Hear, hear," Senator Baal said. "I obviously misjudged you all. Bagayogo and Sanad, I give you both your freedom. From this moment on you're not slaves anymore, you're free men!"

The two men thanked the senator and bowed.

"And as for your children," the senator said, "how can I reward you?"

Ibraheem and Menalik looked at each other.

"Actually," Ibraheem said, "we have a request for Sulaimān (A)."

The most powerful man in the world leaned forward slightly and said, "If it is in my power to grant your wish then it shall be done. Why do you keep saying Alaihi's-salam whenever you say my name?"

"Rasulullah (S) said to always show our love and respect for Prophets s of Allah (SWT) by saying Alaihi's-salam after their name. It means peace be upon you," said Menalik

"Amazing, tell me more. Who is this Rasulullah? Where is he?" Asked Sulaimān (A)

"Rasulullah's name is Prophet Muhammad and."

Before Menalik could finish his sentence Sulaimān's (A) soldiers drew their swords and weapons on Menalik

"Young hero, pick your next words carefully. Where is this Muhammad that claims to be a prophet. I would like to talk to him!" Said Sulaimān (A) as he approached Menalik.

"You can't" said Ibraheem as he stepped up to support his brother. Sulaimān (A) turned to face Ibraheem "Really, why not?"

"Because…. He is not born yet. He is the illiterate prophet that is to come in the end of times."

"Ah yes, it is foretold that a great prophet will come in the end of times and he will be unlettered and he will lead all mankind to all truth. His name is Ahmad" said Sulaimān (A)

"That's him! Muhammad (S) is the Arabic name for Ahmed," said Zaria.

Sulaimān (A) listened intently as the children shared their knowledge of the teachings of Prophet Muhammad (S).

"Tell me, how do you children know the teachings of a Prophet of Elohim that has not been born yet?" (SWT)

"Ah, I can't explain it to you, but just know that all things are possible by the will of God," said Ibraheem

When Ibraheem told him what they wanted Sulaimān (A) first looked surprised and then he laughed.

"You can ask me for anything in the world you like and your wish is to travel with me and Sheba in a ship on the River Jordan?"

The children nodded.

"Then it shall be so," Sulaimān (A) said.

A fortnight later Queen Sheba's royal barge left the quayside and sailed up the River Jordan. The four children were standing at the prow and looked at the mighty river. There were some crocodiles swimming in it and in the distance, they could make out several hippopotami.

"At last," Menalik said, "we can go home.

Ibraheem smiled and nodded.

Zaria turned round and peered at the main deck where a sumptuous meal was being served in front of Sulaimān Ibn Dāwūd (A) and Queen Sheba. They were smiling at each other and chatting happily.

"So that's how this famous love story began," Zaria thought. "And I'm really here with them!"

At that moment Zaria remembered that they had fulfilled the challenge. She laughed and clapped her hands so that the others looked to her. "What a wonderful adventure we've had," she smiled. "I just feel sorry for all the slaves."

Zaria looked at Ibraheem and Menalik with an impish glint in her eye.

"No, wait..." Menalik said.

"I challenge you," Zaria interrupted him, "help me free a thousand slaves."

Whirling stars appeared all around them and in a trice Ibraheem, Menalik and Zaria vanished in front of Adina's eyes. She knew about their secret, though she did wonder where they had gone. Only Sulaimān (A) and Sheba didn't notice anything. They were too busy enjoying their time together and planning not only their own future, but that of the ancient world.

1. Remember when Captain Erythraean was surprised by Zaria's courage to face Jassasah himself. As a Muslim we are taught to only fear Allah.

1. Remember when Ibraheem asked Bagayogo why he was helping? Do you remember his answer? As a Muslim we must always be willing to help those around us that is in need if we can.

1. Remember how Captain Erythraean decided to change his life and go in search of peace and happiness? Always Remember in Islam it is never to late to change your life and strive for a life of peace and happiness for the pleasure of Allah.

Epilogue:

THE JASSASAH HADITH

Amir b. Sharahil Sha'bi Sha'b Hamdan reported that he asked Fatima, daughter of Qais and sister of ad-Dahhak b. Qais and she was the first amongst the emigrant women:

Narrate to me a hadith which you had heard directly from Allah's Messenger (ﷺ) and there is no extra link in between them. She said: Very well, if you like, I am prepared to do that, and he said to her: Well, do It and narrate that to me.

She said: I married the son of Mughira and he was a chosen young man of Quraish at that time, but he fell as a martyr in the first Jihad (fighting) on the side of Allah's Messenger (ﷺ). When I became a widow, 'Abd al-Rahman b. Auf, one amongst the group of the Companions of Allah's Messenger (ﷺ), sent me the proposal of marriage. Allah's Messenger (ﷺ) also sent me such a message for his freed slave Usama b. Zaid. And it had been conveyed to me that Allah's Messenger (ﷺ) had said (about Usama): He who loves me should also love Usama. When Allah's Messenger (ﷺ) talked to me (about this matter), I said: My affairs are in your hand. You may marry me to anyone whom you like.

He said: You better shift now to the house of Umm Sharik, and Umm Sharik was a rich lady from amongst the Ansar. She spent generously for the cause of Allah and entertained guests very hospitably. I said: Well, I will do as you like. He said: Do not do that for Umm Sharik is a woman who is very frequently visited by guests and I do not like that your head may be uncovered or the cloth may be removed from your shank and the strangers may catch sight of them which you abhor. You better shift to the house of your cousin 'Abdullah b. 'Amr b. Umm Maktum and he is a person of the Bani Fihr branch of the Quraish, and he belonged to that tribe (to which Fatima) belonged.

So I shifted to that house, and when my period of waiting was over, I heard the voice of an announcer making an announcement that the prayer would be observed in the mosque (where) congregational prayer (is observed). So I set out towards that mosque and observed prayer along with Allah's Messenger (ﷺ) and I was in the row of the women which was near the row of men.

When Allah's Messenger (ﷺ) had finished his prayer, he sat on the pulpit smiling and said: Every worshipper should keep sitting at his place. He then said: Do you know why I had asked you to assemble? They said: Allah and His Messenger know best. He said: By Allah. I have not made you assemble for exhortation or for a warning, but I have detained you here, for Tamim Dari, a Christian, who came and accepted Islam, told me something, which agrees with what I was telling, you about the Dajjal.

He narrated to me that he had sailed in a ship along with thirty men of Bani Lakhm and Bani Judham and had been tossed by waves in the ocean for a month. Then these (waves) took them (near) the land within the ocean (island) at the time of sunset. They sat in a small side-boat and entered that island.

There was a beast with long thick hair (and because of these) they could not distinguish his face from his back. They said: Woe to you, who can you be? Thereupon it said: I am al-Jassasah. They said: What is al-Jassasah? And it said: O people, go to this person in the monastery as he is very much eager to know about you. He (the narrator) said: When it named a person for us we were afraid of it lest it should be a devil.

Then we hurriedly went on till we came to that monastery and found a well-built person there with his hands tied to his neck and having iron shackles between his two legs up to the ankles. We said: Woe be upon thee, who are you? And he said: You would soon come to know about me. but tell me who are you. We said: We are people from Arabia and we embarked upon a boat but the sea-waves had been driving us for one month and they brought as near this island.

We got Into the side-boats and entered this island and here a beast met us with profusely thick hair and because of the thickness of his hair his face could not be distinguished from his back. We said: Woe be to thee, who are you? It said: I am al- Jassasah. We said: What is al-Jassasah? And it said: You go to this very person in the monastery for he is eagerly waiting for you to know about you.

So we came to you in hot haste fearing that that might be the Devil. He (that chained person) said: Tell me about the date-palm trees of Baisan. We said: About what aspect of theirs do you seek information? He said: I ask you whether these trees bear fruit or not. We said: yes. Thereupon he said: I think these would not bear fruits. He said: Inform me about the lake of Tabariyya? We said: Which aspect of it do you want to know? He said: Is there water in it? They said: There is abundance of water in it. Thereupon he said: I think it would soon become dry. He again said: Inform me about the spring of Zughar. They said: Which aspect of it you want to know? He (the chained person) said: Is there water in it and does it irrigate (the land)? We said to him: Yes, there is abundance of water in it and the inhabitants (of Medina) irrigate (land) with the help of it, He said: Inform me about the unlettered Prophet; what has he done? We said: He has come out from Mecca and has settled In Yathrib (Medina). He said: Do the Arabs fight against him? We said: Yes. He said: How did he deal with them? We informed him that he had overcome those in his neighbourhood and they had submitted themselves before him. Thereupon he said to us: Has it actually happened? We said: Yes.

Thereupon he said: If it is so that is better for them that they should show obedience to him.

I am going to tell you about myself and I am Dajjal and would be soon permitted to get out and so I shall get out and travel in the land, and will not spare any town where I would not stay for forty nights except Mecca and Medina as these two (places) are prohibited (areas) for me and I would not make an attempt to enter any one of these two. An angel with a sword in his hand would confront me and would bar my way and there would be angels to guard every passage leading to it;

then Allah's Messenger (ﷺ) striking the pulpit with the help of the end of his staff said: This implies Taiba meaning Medina. Have I not, told you an account (of the Dajjal) like this? 'The people said: Yes, and this account narrated by Tamim Dari was liked by me for it corroborates the account which I gave to you in regard to him (Dajjal) at Medina and Mecca. Behold he (Dajjal) is in the Syrian sea (Mediterranean) or the Yemen sea (Arabian sea). Nay, on the contrary, he is in the east, he is in the east, he is in the east, and he pointed with his hand towards the east. I (Fatima bint Qais) said: I preserved it in my mind (this narration from Allah's Messenger (ﷺ).

About the Author

Tony Pang is an Old-Fashioned Storyteller hailed by the Anesthesia Technician Survival Guide 2nd Edition as "Smart, Mysterious, and a Performing Poet."

Pang is the humble leader of Vibes of intelligent Creative Essence (VOICE) and has collaborated with Big-House Records, Matt B., Heartspeak Productions, The John Howard Society, the Vancouver Restorative Justice Community, The BCMA, Sepia Players, and was the 1998 prizewinner of the Black Thought Competition for Slam Poets, and the 1998 Writers World Special Achievement Award.

When Pang is not writing or editing, he can be found working on his small farm

www.ingramcontent.com/pod-product-compliance
Lightning Source LLC
Chambersburg PA
CBHW051235210726
48290CB00003B/973